Series Editor: Rosalind Kerven

© 1996 Rigby Education
Published by Rigby Interactive Library,
an imprint of Rigby Education,
division of Reed Elsevier, Inc.
500 Coventry Lane,
Crystal Lake, IL 60014

Printed in Hong Kong

00 99 98 97 96
10 9 8 7 6 5 4 3 2 1

Library of Congress Cataloging-in-Publication Data

Potter, Tessa.
     Beowulf and the dragon / retold by Tessa Potter;
  illustrated by Simon Noyes; series editor, Rosalind Kerven.
      p. cm. — (Myths and legends (Crystal Lake, Ill.))
    "First published in Great Britain by Heinemann Library"—T.p.
verso.
    Summary: A brief retelling of the Anglo-Saxon epic about the
heroic efforts of King Beowulf of Geatland to save his people from a
terrible dragon.
    ISBN 1-57572-017-5 (lib.)
     1. Beowulf—Adaptations. [1. Beowulf. 2. Folklore—England.]
I. Noyes, Simon, ill. II. Title. III. Series.
PZ8.1.P8Be   1996
    398'.2'0942'02—dc20   95-38246

Acknowledgments
Title page and border illustration, pp. 2–3: Nadine Wickendon;
map, p. 2: Dave Bowyer;
photographs, p. 3 (top, bottom left): Michael Holform, (bottom right): C.M. Dixon

Beowulf and the Dragon

Retold by Tessa Potter
Illustrated by Simon Noyes
Series Editor: Rosalind Kerven

About the Anglo-Saxons

"Beowulf" is an Anglo-Saxon poem.
It was probably written in England
about 1,200 years ago.
The Angles and the Saxons were
invaders and settlers from other
countries who brought their legends
to England.
"Beowulf" takes place in
the Land of the Geats,
in what is now Sweden.

Map of Anglo Saxon Lands

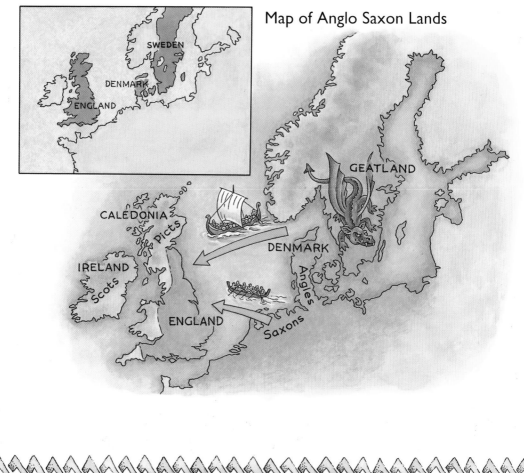

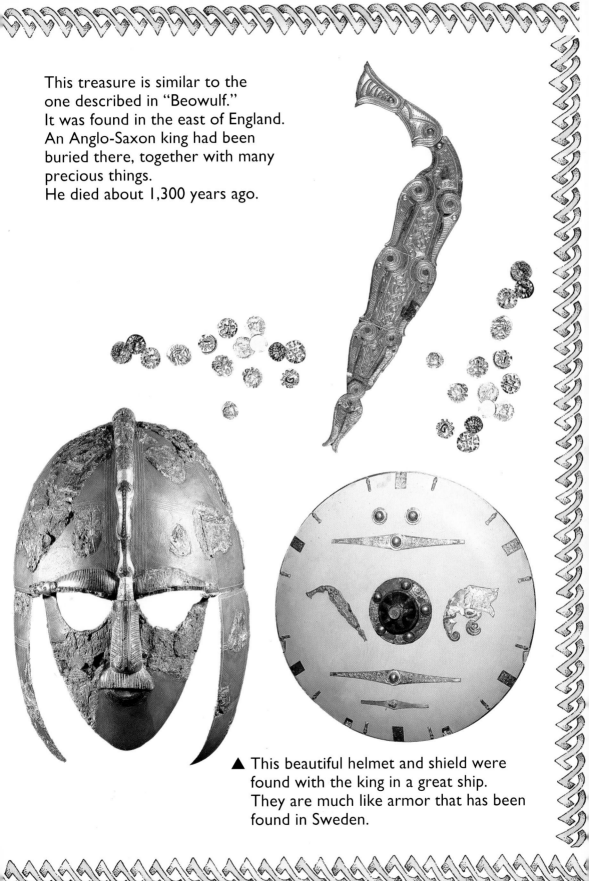

This treasure is similar to the
one described in "Beowulf."
It was found in the east of England.
An Anglo-Saxon king had been
buried there, together with many
precious things.
He died about 1,300 years ago.

▲ This beautiful helmet and shield were
found with the king in a great ship.
They are much like armor that has been
found in Sweden.

Long ago, a fierce dragon came to Geatland.
The dragon made its home in a dark cave
at the edge of the sea.
Inside that cave, the dragon found a hoard of
golden treasure and fine weapons.

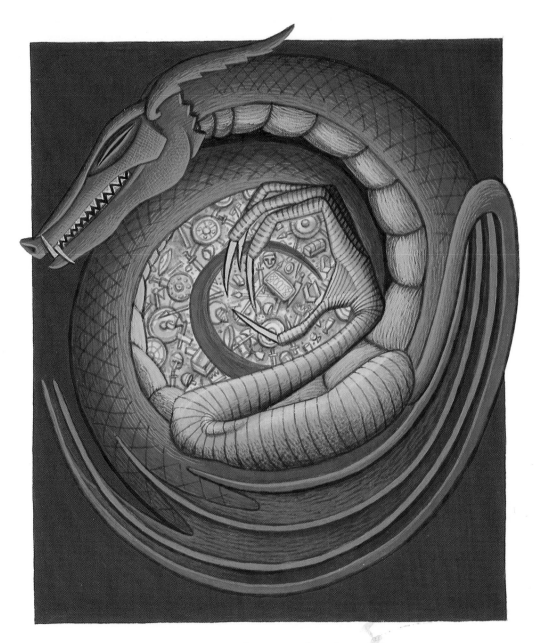

The dragon stood guard over the hoard.
He coiled his body around the treasure.
The dragon grew bigger and bigger until
only a tiny glimmer of gold could be seen.
No one came near the cave for
three hundred years.

Then one day, a man found the cave.

He crept inside.

He saw a glimmer of gold under the dragon.

While the dragon slept,

the man stole a golden cup.

The dragon woke up and smelled the man.
He saw footprints in the sand and
found that a piece of the treasure was missing.
He knew that his gold would never be safe again.
The dragon roared a great roar.
He spat fire and smoke in his fury.

That night the dragon flew over
Geatland, looking for the thief.
He burned down houses and villages.
He burned down trees and fields.
His anger was terrible.
Wherever he flew, his hot breath
spread flames over the ground.

8

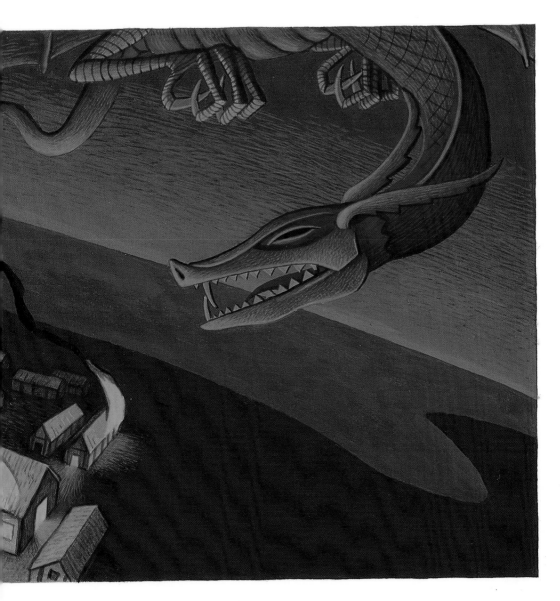

People ran for their lives,
but no one could escape the dragon's fire.
Every night he left his cave
and flew over the land,
burning everything he saw.
Even the king's great hall
was burned to the ground.

The king's name was Beowulf.
He had ruled Geatland for fifty years.
He had won many battles
and destroyed terrible monsters.
He was old now, but he knew
he had one last battle to fight.
He must kill this dragon and save his people.

King Beowulf took a great shield of iron.
Only iron could protect him from the flames.
He chose eleven of his bravest soldiers
to ride with him.
One of these was his young relative, Wiglaf.

The man who had stolen the dragon's treasure
led the way to the dragon's cave.
They followed a terrible trail
of black fields and burned forests.
At last they came to a high cliff.
The man pointed to a cave in the rocks below.
Steam and smoke rose up from the ground.

King Beowulf took his sword and his shield
and ran down to the rocks.
He cried out in a loud voice,
"Come out evil one, killer-by-night.
I have come to destroy you and win the gold.
You will no longer bring death to my people."

The dragon heard Beowulf and flew out.
The great beast stood on the sand,
hissing and lashing his tail.
The scales on his back glowed red and golden.
Flames poured from his mouth.
The ground shook.

14

King Beowulf was not afraid.

He moved closer holding his shield high.

He lifted his sword and struck the dragon hard.

The dragon screamed and spat more fire.

The fire wrapped Beowulf in a ball of flames.

Even the iron shield began to melt.

The soldiers on the cliff saw the flames
around Beowulf and began to run away.
Wiglaf called after them, "How can you leave
our king when he needs us most?
Has he not given us gold and fine weapons?
Did we not promise to be brave and loyal
and swear to help him always?"
But the soldiers were afraid of the dragon.

Only Wiglaf ran down to help the king.
His wooden shield burst into flames as he got near,
but he did not turn back.
The old king found new strength
with young Wiglaf at his side.
He lifted his sword again to kill the dragon.
But this time the sword broke.

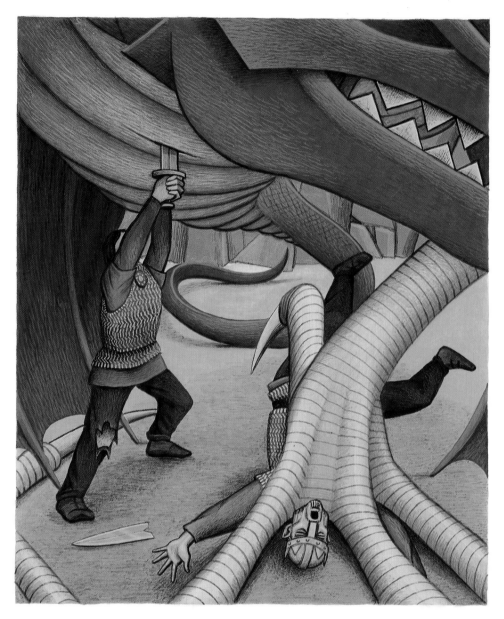

The dragon lifted its great claws and
tore at Beowulf, wounding him terribly.
At that moment, Wiglaf crept under the beast
and struck the dragon from below.
The dragon's blood spilled onto the ground
and the fierce flames died down.

Now, with his last strength, King Beowulf took his
knife and cut the beast in two.
Then he staggered to the rocks.
His life was nearly over, but the dragon was dead,
and his people were saved.

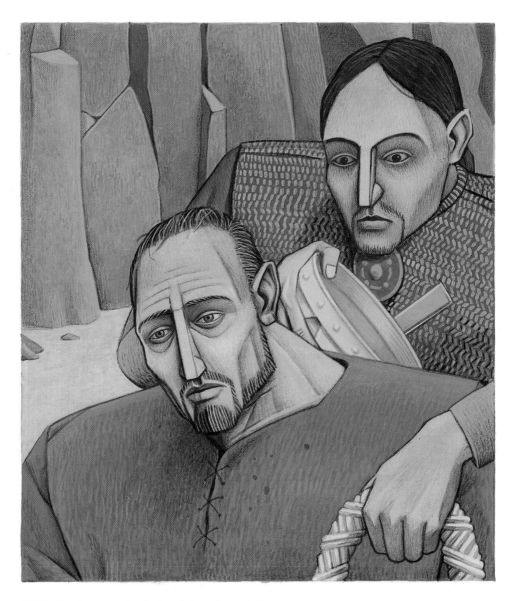

Wiglaf ran to his king's side.

"I am dying," said Beowulf.

"Take my helmet and battle armor, brave Wiglaf.

And take this golden collar.

I have no son of my own,

so you shall be the next King of the Geats.

Now before I die, let me see the dragon's gold."

Wiglaf ran to the dragon's cave.
He brought out all the treasure he could carry
and laid it on the rocks.
Golden cups and rings, swords and helmets,
gleaming and glistening in the sunlight.
The great king gazed at them,
and then he died.

They carried King Beowulf's body to the cliff top.
Around him they hung shields and weapons
from the dragon's hoard.
They made ready a great funeral fire.
The torch was lit.
For many miles around,
the people of Geatland saw the funeral fire
and knew that their good king was dead.

Then Wiglaf ordered that a high stone barrow
be built around the ashes of their king.
And in the barrow, they laid the dragon's gold.
"Our noble king lost his life
to win this gold," said Wiglaf.
"Let it return with him to the darkness."

And so Beowulf's Barrow was made,
a great mound of stones high on the cliff top.
The stones shone white in the sun.
All those who sailed on the sea below
looked up and remembered Beowulf.
Beowulf the gold giver, Beowulf the great soldier,
Beowulf the Dragon Killer.